JOHN
BANVILLE

THE NEWTON LETTER

PICADOR

This edition published 1999 by Picador
an imprint of Pan Macmillan Ltd
Pan Macmillan, 20 New Wharf Road, London NI 9RR
Basingstoke and Oxford
Associated companies throughout the world
www.panmacmillan.com

ISBN 0 330 37235 1

35798642

A CIP catalogue record for this book is available from
the British Library.

Printed and bound in Great Britain by
Mackays of Chatham plc, Chatham, Kent

to Vincent Lawrence

*I seem to have been only as a boy playing on the seashore,
and diverting myself in now and then finding a smoother
pebble or a prettier shell than ordinary, whilst
the great ocean of truth lay all undiscovered before me.*

Sir Isaac Newton

WORDS FAIL ME, Clio. How did you
track me down, did I leave bloodstains in the snow? I
won't try to apologise. Instead, I want simply to explain,
so that we both might understand. Simply! I like that.
No, I'm not sick, I have not had a breakdown. I am,
you might say, I might say, in retirement from life.
Temporarily.

I have abandoned my book. You'll think me mad.
Seven years I gave to it—seven years! How can I make
you understand that such a project is now for me impossible, when I don't really understand it myself? Shall
I say, I've lost my faith in the primacy of text? Real
people keep getting in the way now, objects, landscapes
even. Everything ramifies. I think for example of the

1

first time I went down to Ferns. From the train I looked at the shy back-end of things, drainpipes and broken windows, straggling gardens with their chorus lines of laundry, a man bending to a spade. Out on Killiney bay a white sail was tilted at an angle to the world, a white cloud was slowly cruising the horizon. What has all this to do with anything? Yet such remembered scraps seem to me abounding in significance. They are at once commonplace and unique, like clues at the scene of a crime. But everything that day was still innocent as the blue sky itself, so what do they prove? Perhaps just that: the innocence of things, their non-complicity in our affairs. All the same I'm convinced those drainpipes and that cloud require me far more desperately than I do them. You see my difficulty.

I might have written to you last September, before I fled, with some bland excuse. You would have understood, certainly at least you would have sympathised. But Clio, dear Cliona, you have been my teacher and my friend, my inspiration, for too long, I couldn't lie to you. Which doesn't mean I know what the truth is, and how to tell it to you. I'm confused. I feel ridiculous and melodramatic, and comically exposed. I have shinned up to this high perch and can't see how to get down, and of the spectators below, some are embarrassed and the rest are about to start laughing.

I S H O U L D N ' T H A V E gone down there. It was the name that attracted me. Fern House! I expected—Oh, I expected all sorts of things. It turned out to be a big gloomy pile with ivy and peeling walls and a smashed fanlight over the door, the kind of place where you picture a mad stepdaughter locked up in the attic. There was an avenue of sycamores and then the road falling away down the hill to the village. In the distance I could see the smoke of the town, and beyond that again a sliver of sea. I suppose, thinking about it, that *was* much what I expected. To look at, anyway.

Two women met me in the garden. One was large and blonde, the other a tall girl with brown arms, wearing a tattered straw sun hat. The blonde spoke: they had seen me coming. She pointed down the hill road. I assumed she was the woman of the house, the girl in the sun hat her sister perhaps. I pictured them, vigilantly silent, watching me toiling toward them, and I felt for some reason flattered. Then the girl took off her hat, and she was not a girl, but a middle-aged woman. I had got them nearly right, but the wrong way round. This was Charlotte Lawless, and the big blonde girl was Ottilie, her niece.

The lodge, as they called it, stood on the roadside at the end of the drive. Once there had been a wall and a high pillared gate, but all that was long gone, the way of other glories. The door screeched. A bedroom and a parlour, a tiny squalid kitchen, a tinier bathroom. Ottilie followed me amiably from room to room, her hands stuck in the back pockets of her trousers. Mrs Lawless waited in the front doorway. I opened the kitchen cupboard: cracked mugs and mouse-shit. There was a train back to town in an hour, I would make it if I hurried. Mrs Lawless fingered the brim of her sun hat and considered the sycamores. Of the three of us only blonde Ottilie was not embarrassed. Stepping past Charlotte in the doorway I caught her milky smell—and heard myself offering her a month's rent in advance.

What possessed me? Ferns was hardly that Woolsthorpe of my vague dreams, where, shut away from the pestilence of college life, I would put the final touches to my own *Principia*. Time is different in the country. There were moments when I thought I would panic, stranded in the midst of endless afternoons. Then there was the noise, a constant row, heifers bellowing, tractors growling, the dogs baying all night. Things walked on the roof, scrabbled under the floor. There was a nest of blackbirds in the lilacs outside the parlour window where I tried to work. The whole bush shook with their quarrelling. And one night a herd of something, cows, horses, I don't know, came and milled around on the lawn, breathing and nudging, like a mob gathering for the attack.

But the weather that late May was splendid, sunny and still, and tinged with sadness. I killed whole days rambling the fields. I had brought guidebooks to trees and birds, but I couldn't get the hang of them. The illustrations would not match up with the real specimens before me. Every bird looked like a starling. I soon got discouraged. Perhaps that explains the sense I had of being an interloper. Amid those sunlit scenes I felt detached, as if I myself were a mere idea, a stylised and subtly inaccurate illustration of something that was only real elsewhere. Even the pages of my manuscript, when I sat worriedly turning them over, had an unfamiliar look, as if they had been written, not by someone else, but by another version of myself.

Remember that mad letter Newton wrote to John Locke in September of 1693, accusing the philosopher out of the blue of being immoral, and a Hobbist, and of having tried to embroil him with women? I picture old Locke pacing the great garden at Oates, eyebrows leaping higher and higher as he goggles at these wild charges. I wonder if he felt the special pang which I feel reading the subscription: *I am your most humble and unfortunate servant, Is. Newton.* It seems to me to express better than anything that has gone before it Newton's pain and anguished bafflement. I compare it to the way a few weeks later he signed, with just the stark surname, another, and altogether different, letter. What happened in the interval, what knowledge dawned on him?

We have speculated a great deal, you and I, on his nervous collapse late in that summer of '93. He was fifty, his greatest work was behind him, the *Principia* and the gravity laws, the discoveries in optics. He was giving himself up more and more to interpretative study of the Bible, and to that darker work in alchemy which so embarrasses his biographers (cf. Popov *et al.*). He was a great man now, his fame was assured, all Europe honoured him. But his life as a scientist was over. The process of lapidescence had begun: the world was turning him into a monument to himself. He was cold, arrogant, lonely. He was still obsessively jealous—his hatred of Hooke was to endure, indeed to intensify, even beyond the death of his old adversary. He was—

Look at me, writing history; old habits die hard. All I meant to say is that the book was as good as done, I had only to gather up a few loose ends, and write the conclusion—but in those first weeks at Ferns something started to go wrong. It was only as yet what the doctors call a vague general malaise. I was concentrating, with morbid fascination, on the chapter I had devoted to his breakdown and those two letters to Locke. Was that a lump I felt there, a little, hard, painless lump . . . ?

Mostly of course such fears seemed ridiculous. There were even moments when the prospect of finishing the thing merged somehow with my new surroundings into a grand design. I recall one day when I was in, appropriately enough, the orchard. The sun was shining, the trees were in blossom. It would be a splendid book, fresh and clean as this bright scene before me. The academies would be stunned, you would be proud of me, and Cambridge would offer me a big job. I felt an extraordinary sense of purity, of tender innocence. Thus Newton himself must have stood one fine morning in his mother's garden at Woolsthorpe, as the ripe apples dropped about his head. I turned, hearing a violent thrashing of small branches. Edward Lawless stepped sideways through a gap in the hedge, kicking a leg behind him to free a snagged trouser cuff. There was a leaf in his hair.

I had seen him about the place, but this was the first time we had met. His face was broad and pallid, his blue eyes close-set and restless. He was not a very big man, but he gave an impression of, how would I say, of volume. He had a thick short neck, and wide shoulders that rolled as he walked, as if he had constantly to deal with large soft obstacles in air. Standing beside him I could hear him breathing, like a man poised between one lumbering run and another. For all his rough bulk, though, there was in his eyes a look, preoccupied, faintly pained, like the look you see in those pearl and ink photographs of doomed Georgian poets. His flaxen hair, greying nicely at the temples, was a burnished helmet; I itched to reach out and remove the laurel leaf tangled in it. We stood together in the drenched grass, looking at the sky and trying to think of something to say. He commended the weather. He jingled change in his pocket. He coughed. There was a shout far off, and then from farther off an answering call. "Aha," he said, relieved, "the rat men!" and plunged away through the gap in the hedge. A moment later his head appeared again, swinging above the grassy bank that bounded the orchard. Always I think of him like this, skulking behind hedges, or shambling across a far field, rueful and somehow angry, like a man with a hangover trying to remember last night's crimes.

I walked back along the path under the apple trees and came out on the lawn, a cropped field really. Two figures in wellingtons and long black buttonless overcoats appeared around the side of the house. One had a long-handled brush over his shoulder, the other carried a red bucket. I stopped and watched them pass before me in the spring sunshine, and all at once I was assailed by an image of catastrophe, stricken things scurrying in circles, the riven pelts, the convulsions, the agonised eyes gazing into the empty sky or through the sky into the endlessness. I hurried off to the lodge, to my work. But the sense of harmony and purpose I had felt in the orchard was gone. I saw something move outside on the grass. I thought it was the blackbirds out foraging, for the lilacs were still. But it was a rat.

In fact, it wasn't a rat. In fact in all my time at Ferns I never saw sign of a rat. It was only the idea.

The campus postman, an asthmatic Lapp, has just brought me a letter from Ottilie. Now I'm really found out. She says she got my address from you. Clio, Clio . . . But I'm glad, I won't deny it. Less in what she says than in the Lilliputian scrawl itself, aslant from corner to corner of the flimsy blue sheets, do I glimpse something of the real she, her unhandiness and impetuosity, her inviolable innocence. She wants me to lend her the fare to come and visit me! I can see us, staggering through the snowdrifts, ranting and weeping, embracing in our furs like lovelorn polar bears.

She came down to the lodge the day after I moved in, bringing me a bowl of brown eggs. She wore corduroy trousers and a shapeless homemade sweater. Her blonde hair was tied at the back with a rubber band. Pale eyebrows and pale blue eyes gave her a scrubbed look. With her hands thrust in her pockets she stood and smiled at me. Hers was the brave brightness of all big awkward girls.

"Grand eggs," I said.

We considered them a moment in thoughtful silence.

"Charlotte rears them," she said. "Hens, I mean."

I went back to the box of books I had been unpacking. She hesitated, glancing about. The little square table by the window was strewn with my papers. Was I writing a book, or what?—as if such a thing were hardly defensible. I told her. "Newton," she said, frowning. "The fellow that the apple fell on his head and he discovered gravity?"

She sat down.

She was twenty-four. Her father had been Charlotte Lawless's brother. With his wife beside him one icy night when Ottilie was ten he had run his car into a wall—"that wall, see, down there"—and left the girl an orphan. She wanted to go to university. To study what? She shrugged. She just wanted to go to university. Her voice, incongruous coming out of that big frame, was light and vibrant as an oboe, a singer's voice, and I pictured her, this large unlovely girl, standing in a preposterous gown before the tiered snowscape of an orchestra, her little fat hands clasped, pouring forth a storm of disconsolate song.

Where did I live in Dublin? Had I a flat? What was it like? "Why did you come down to this dump?" I told her, to finish my book, and then frowned at the papers curling gently in the sunlight on the table. Then I noticed how the sycamores were stirring faintly, almost surreptitiously in the bright air, like dancers practising steps in their heads, and something in me too pirouetted briefly, and yes, I said, yes, to finish my book. A shadow fell in the doorway. A tow-haired small boy stood there, with his hands at his back, watching us. His ancient gaze, out of a putto's pale eyes, was unnerving. Ottilie sighed, and rose abruptly, and without another glance at me took the child's hand and departed.

I WAS born down there, in the south, you knew that. The best memories I have of the place are of departures from it. I'm thinking of Christmas trips to Dublin when I was a child, boarding the train in the dark and watching through the mist of my breath on the window the frost-bound landscape assembling as the dawn came up. At a certain spot every time, I can see it still, day would at last achieve itself. The place was a river bend, where the train slowed down to cross a red metal bridge. Beyond the river a flat field ran to the edge of a wooded hill, and at the foot of the hill there was a house, not very big, solitary and square, with a steep roof. I would gaze at that silent house and wonder, in a hunger of curiosity, what lives were lived there. Who stacked that firewood, hung that holly wreath, left those tracks in the hoarfrost on the hill? I can't express the odd aching pleasure of that moment. I knew, of course, that those hidden lives wouldn't be much different from my own. But that was the point. It wasn't the exotic I was after, but the *ordinary*, that strangest and most elusive of enigmas.

Now I had another house to gaze at, and wonder about, with something of the same remote prurience. The lodge was like a sentry box. It stood, what, a hundred, two hundred yards from the house, yet I couldn't look out my window without spotting some bit of business going on. The acoustics of the place too afforded an alarming intimacy. I could clearly hear the frequent cataclysms of the upstairs lavatory, and my day began with the pips for the morning news on the radio in Charlotte Lawless's kitchen. Then I would see Charlotte herself, in wellingtons and an old cardigan, hauling out a bucket of feed to the henhouse. Next comes Ottilie, in a sleepy trance, with the child by the hand. He is off to school. He carries his satchel like a hunchback's hump. Edward is last, I am at work before I spy him about his mysterious business. It all has the air of a pastoral mime, with the shepherd's wife and the shepherd, and Cupid and the maid, and, scribbling within a crystal cave, myself, a haggard-eyed Damon.

I had them spotted for patricians from the start. The big house, Edward's tweeds, Charlotte's fine-boned slender grace that the dowdiest of clothes could not mask, even Ottilie's awkwardness, all this seemed the unmistakable stamp of their class. Protestants, of course, landed, the land gone now to gombeen men and compulsory purchase, the family fortune wasted by tax, death duties, inflation. But how bravely, how beautifully they bore their losses! Observing them, I understood that breeding such as theirs is a preparation not for squiredom itself, but for that distant day, which for the Lawlesses had arrived, when the trappings of glory are gone and only style remains. All nonsense, of course, but to me, product of a post-peasant Catholic upbringing, they appeared perfected creatures. Oh, don't accuse me of snobbery. This was something else, a fascination before the spectacle of pure refinement. Shorn of the dull encumbrances of wealth and power, they were free to be purely what they were. The irony was, the form of life their refinement took was wholly familiar to me: wellington boots, henhouses, lumpy sweaters. Familiar, but, ah, transfigured. The nicety of tone and gesture to which I might aspire, they achieved by instinct, unwittingly. Their ordinariness was inimitable.

Sunday mornings were a gala performance at Ferns. At twenty to ten, the bells pealing down in the village, a big old-fashioned motor car would feel its way out of the garage. They are off to church. An hour later they return, minus Edward, with Charlotte at the wheel. Wisps of tiny music from the radio in the kitchen come to me. Charlotte is getting the dinner ready—no, she is preparing a light lunch. Not for them surely the midday feeds of my childhood, the mighty roast, the steeped marrowfat peas, the block of runny ice-cream on its cool perch on the bathroom windowsill. Edward tramps up the hill, hands in his pockets, shoulders rolling. In front of the house he pauses, looks at the broken fanlight, and then goes in, the door shuts, the train moves on, over the bridge.

My illusions about them soon began, if not to crumble, then to modify. One day I struck off past the orchard into the lands at the back of the house. All round were the faint outlines of what must once have been an ornate garden. Here was a pond, the water an evil green, overhung by a sadness of willows. I waded among hillocks of knee-high grass, feeling watched. The day was hot, with a burning breeze. Everything swayed. A huge bumble bee blundered past my ear. When I looked back, the only sign of the house was a single chimney pot against the sky. I found myself standing on the ruins of a tennis court. A flash of reflected sunlight caught my eye. In a hollow at the far side of the court there was a long low glasshouse. I stumbled down the bank, as others in another time must have stumbled, laughing, after a white ball rolling inexorably into the future. The door of the glasshouse made a small sucking sound when I opened it. The heat was a soft slap in the face. Row upon row of clay pots on trestle tables ran the length of the place, like an exercise in perspective, converging at the far end on the figure of Charlotte Lawless standing with her back to me. She wore sandals and a wide green

skirt, a white shirt, her tattered sun hat. I spoke, and
she turned, startled. A pair of spectacles hung on a cord
about her neck. Her fingers were caked with clay. She
dabbed the back of a wrist to her forehead. I noticed the
tiny wrinkles around her eyes, the faint down on her
upper lip.

I said I hadn't known the hothouse was here, I was
impressed, she must be an enthusiastic gardener. I was
babbling. She looked at me carefully. "It's how we make
our living," she said. I apologised, I wasn't sure for
what, and then laughed, and felt foolish. There are people to whom you feel compelled to explain yourself. "I
got lost," I said, "in the garden, believe it or not, and
then I saw you here, and..." She was still watching
me, hanging on my words; I wondered if she were perhaps hard of hearing. The possibility was oddly touching. Or was it simply that she wasn't really listening?
Her face was empty of all save a sense of something
withheld. She made me think of someone standing on
tiptoe behind a glass barrier, every part of her, eyes,
lips, the gloves that she clutches, straining to become
the radiant smile that awaits the beloved's arrival. She
was all potential. On the bench where she had been
working lay an open secateurs, and a cut plant with
purple flowers.

We went among the tables, wading through a dead
and standing pool of air, and she explained her work,
naming the plants, the strains and hybrids, in a neutral
voice. Mostly it was plain commercial stuff, apple tree-

lets, flower bulbs, vegetables, but there were some strange things, with strange pale stalks, and violent blossoms, and bearded fruit dangling among the glazed, still leaves. Her father had started the business, and she had taken it over when her brother was killed. "We still trade as Grainger Nurseries." I nodded dully. The heat, the sombre hush, the contrast between the stillness here and the windy tumult pressing against the glass all around us, provoked in me a kind of excited apprehension, as if I were being led, firmly, but with infinite tact, into peril. Ranked colours thronged me round, crimson, purples, and everywhere green and more green, glabrous and rubbery and somehow ferocious. "In Holland," she said, "in the seventeenth century, a nurseryman could sell a new strain of tulip for twenty thousand pounds." It had the flat sound of something read into a recorder. She looked at me, her hands folded, waiting for my comment. I smiled, and shook my head, trying to look amazed. We reached the door. The summer breeze seemed a hurricane after the silence within. My shirt clung to my back. I shivered. We walked a little way down a path under an arch of rhododendrons. The tangled arthritic branches let in scant light, and there was a smell of mossy rot reminiscent of the tang of damp flesh. Then at once, unaccountably, we were at the rear of the house. I was confused; the garden had surreptitiously taken me in a circle. Charlotte murmured something, and walked away. On the drive under the sycamores I paused and looked back. The house was impassive, except where a curtain in an open upstairs window waved frantically in the breeze. What did I expect? Some revelation? A face watching me through sky-reflecting glass, a voice calling my name? There was nothing—but something had happened, all the same.

The child's name was Michael. I couldn't fit him to the Lawlesses. True, he was given, like Edward, to skulking. I would come upon him in the lanes roundabout, poking in the hedge and muttering to himself, or just standing, with his hands behind him as if hiding something, waiting for me to pass by. Sitting with a book under a tree in the orchard one sunny afternoon, I looked up to find him perched among the branches, studying me. Another time, towards twilight, I spotted him on the road, gazing off intently at something below the brow of the hill where he stood. He had not heard me behind him, and I paused, wondering what it was that merited such rapt attention. Then with a pang I heard it, rising through the stillness of evening, the tinny music of a carnival in the village below.

One evening Edward stopped at the lodge on his way up from the village. He had the raw look of a man lately dragged out of bed and thrust under a cold tap, his eyes were red-rimmed, his hair lank. He hummed and hawed, scuffing the gravel of the roadside, and then abruptly said: "Come up and have a bite to eat." I think that was the first time I had been inside the house. It was dim, and faintly musty. There was a hurley stick in the umbrella stand, and withered daffodils in a vase on the hall table. In an alcove a clock feathered the silence and let drop a single wobbly chime. Edward paused to consult a pocket watch, frowning. In the fusty half-light his face had the grey sheen of putty. He hiccupped softly.

Dinner was in the big whitewashed kitchen at the back of the house. I had expected a gaunt dining-room, linen napkins with a faded initial, a bit of old silver negligently laid. And it was hardly dinner, more a high tea, with cold cuts and limp lettuce, and a bottle of salad cream the colour of gruel. The tablecloth was plastic. Charlotte and Ottilie were already halfway through their meal. Charlotte looked in silence for a moment at my midriff, and I knew at once I shouldn't have come. Ottilie set a place for me. The barred window looked out on a vegetable garden, and then a field, and then the blue haze of distant woods. Sunlight through the leaves of a chestnut tree in the yard was a ceaseless shift and flicker in the corner of my eye. Edward began to tell a yarn he had heard in the village, but got muddled, and sat staring blearily at his plate, breathing. Someone coughed. Ottilie pursed her lips and began to whistle silently. Charlotte with an abrupt spastic movement turned to me and in a loud voice said:

"Do you think we'll give up neutrality?"

"Give up . . . ?" The topic was in the papers. "Well, I don't know, I—"

"Yes, tell us now," Edward said, suddenly stirring himself and thrusting his great bull head at me, "tell us what you think, I'm very interested, we're all very interested, aren't we all very interested? A man like you would know all about these things."

"I think we'd be very—"

"Down here of course we haven't a clue. Crowd of bog-trotters!" He grinned, snorting softly and pawing the turf.

"I think we'd be very unwise to give it up," I said.

"And what about that power station they want to put up down there at Carnsore? Bloody bomb, blow us all up, some clown with a hangover press the wrong button, we won't need the Russians. What?" He was looking at Charlotte. She had not spoken. "Well what's wrong with being ordinary," he said, "like any other country, having an army and defending ourselves? Tell me what's wrong with that." He pouted at us, a big resentful baby.

"What about Switzerland?" Ottilie said; she giggled.

"Switzerland? *Switzerland?* Ha. Milkmen and chocolate factories, and, what was it the fellow said, cuckoo clocks." He turned his red-rimmed gaze on me again. "Too many damn neutrals," he said darkly.

Charlotte sighed, and looked up from her plate at last.

"Edward," she said, without emphasis. He did not take his eyes off me, but the light went out in his face, and for a moment I almost felt sorry for him. "Not that I give a damn anyway," he muttered, and meekly took up his spoon. So much for current affairs.

I cursed myself for being there, and yet I was agog. A trapdoor had been lifted briefly on dim thrashing forms, and now it was shut again. I watched Edward covertly. The sot. He had brought me here for an alibi for his drinking, or to forestall recriminations. I saw the whole thing now, of course: he was a waster, Charlotte kept the place going, everything had been a mistake, even the child. It all fitted, the rueful look and the glazed eye, the skulking, the silences, the tension, that sense I had been aware of from the beginning of being among people facing away from me, intent on something I couldn't see. Even the child's air of sullen autonomy was explained. I looked at Charlotte's fine head, her slender neck, that hand resting by her plate. Leaf-shadow stirred on the table like the shimmer of tears. How could I let her know that I understood everything? The child came in, wrapped in a white bath-towel. His hair was wet, plastered darkly on his skull. When he saw me he drew back, then stepped forward, frowning, a robed and kiss-curled miniature Caesar. Charlotte held out her hand and he went to her. Ottilie winked at him. Edward wore a crooked leer, as if a smile aimed at the centre of his face had landed just wide of the target. Michael mumbled goodnight and departed, shutting the door with both hands on the knob. I turned to Charlotte eagerly. "Your son," I said, in a voice that fairly throbbed, "your son is very . . ." and then floundered, hearing I suppose the tiny tinkle of a warning bell. There was a silence. Charlotte blushed. Suddenly I felt depressed, and . . . prissy, that's the word. What did I know, that gave me the right to judge them? I shouldn't be here at all. I ate a leaf of lettuce, at my back that great rooted blossomer, before me the insistent enigma of other people. I would stay out of their way, keep to the lodge—return to Dublin even. But I knew I wouldn't. Some large lesson seemed laid out here for me.

Ottilie came with me out on the step. She said nothing, but smiled, at once amused and apologetic. And then, I don't know why, the idea came to me. Michael wasn't their child: he was, of course, hers.

THANKS for the latest Popov, it arrived today. Very sly you are, Cliona—but a library of Popovs would not goad me into publishing. I met him once, an awful little man with ferret eyes and a greasy suit. Reminded me of an embalmer. Which, come to think of it, is apt. I like his disclaimer: *Before the phenomenon of Isaac Newton, the historian, like Freud when he came to contemplate Leonardo, can only shake his head and retire with as much good grace as he can muster.* Then out come the syringe and the formalin. That is what I was doing too, embalming old N.'s big corpse, only I *did* have the grace to pop off before the deathshead grin was properly fixed.

Newton was the greatest genius that science has produced. Well, who would deny it? He was still in his twenties

25

when he cracked the code of the world's working. Single-handed he invented science: before him it had all been wizardry and sweaty dreams and brilliant blundering. You may say, as Newton himself said, that he saw so far because he had the shoulders of giants to stand on: but you might as well say that without his mother and father he would not have been born, which is true all right, but what does it signify? Anyway, when he defined the gravity laws he swept away that whole world of giants and other hobgoblins. Oh yes, you can see, can't you, the outline of what my book would have been, a celebration of action, of the scientist as hero, a gleeful acceptance of Pandora's fearful disclosures, wishy-washy medievalism kicked out and the age of reason restored. But would you believe that all this, this Popovian Newton–as–the–greatest–scientist–the–world–has–known, now makes me feel slightly sick? Not that I think any of it untrue, in the sense that it is fact. It's just that another kind of truth has come to seem to me more urgent, although, for the mind, it is nothing compared to the lofty verities of science.

Newton himself, I believe, saw something of the matter in that strange summer of 1693. You know the story, of how his little dog Diamond overturned a candle in his rooms at Cambridge one early morning, and started a fire which destroyed a bundle of his papers, and how the loss deranged his mind. All rubbish, of course, even the dog is a fiction, yet I find myself imagining him, a fifty-year-old public man, standing aghast in the midst of the smoke and the flying smuts with the singed pug pressed in his arms. The joke is, it's not the loss of the precious papers that will drive him temporarily crazy, but the simple fact that *it doesn't matter*. It might be his life's work gone, the *Principia* itself, the *Opticks*, the whole bang lot, and still it wouldn't mean a thing. Tears spring from his eyes, the dog licks them off his chin. A colleague comes running, shirt-tails out. The great man is pulled into the corridor, white with shock and stumping like a peg-leg. Someone beats out the flames. Someone else asks what has been lost. Newton's mouth opens and a word like a stone falls out: *Nothing*. He notices details, early morning light through a window, his rescuer's one unshod foot and yellow toenails, the velvet blackness of burnt paper. He smiles. His fellows look at one another.

It had needed no candle flame, it was already ashes. Why else had he turned to deciphering Genesis and dabbling in alchemy? Why else did he insist again and again that science had cost him too dearly, that, given his life to live over, he would have nothing to do with physics? It wasn't modesty, no one could accuse him of that. The fire, or whatever the real conflagration was, had shown him something terrible and lovely, like flame itself. *Nothing*. The word reverberates. He broods on it as on some magic emblem whose other face is not to be seen and yet is emphatically there. For the nothing automatically signifies the everything. He does not know what to do, what to think. He no longer knows how to live.

There was no fiery revelation to account for *my* crisis of faith; there was not even what could properly be called a crisis. Only, I wasn't working now. The month of June went by and I had not put pen to paper. But I was no longer worried—just the opposite. It was like the passing away of a stubborn illness. You don't notice the gradual calming of the blood, the cleared head, the limbs' new strength, you are aware only of waiting quietly, confidently, for life to start up again. You won't believe me, I know: how could I drop seven years of work, just like that? Newton was my life, not these dull pale people in their tumbledown house in the hollow heart of the country. But I didn't see it as this stark alternative: things take a definite and simple shape only in retrospect. At the time I had only a sense of lateral drift. My papers lay untouched on the table by the window, turning yellow in the sunlight, when my eye fell on them I felt impatience and a vague resentment; my real attention was elsewhere, suspended, ready to give itself with a glad cry to what was coming next.

What came was unexpected.

Consider: a day in June, birds, breezes, flying clouds, the smell of approaching rain. Lunchtime. In the kitchen the stove squats in a hot sulk after its labours, the air is dense with the smoke of burnt fat. A knock.

I drag open the door, cursing silently. Ottilie is standing outside with the child unconscious in her arms.

He had fallen out of a tree. A cut on his forehead was bleeding. I took him from her. He was heavier than I expected, and limp as death, it seemed he might pour through my fingers into a pale puddle on the floor. I felt fright, and a curious faint disgust. I put him on an old horsehair sofa and he coughed and opened his eyes. At first there was only the whites, then the pupils slid down, like something awful coming down in a lift. His face was translucent marble, with violet shadows under the eyes. A large bruise was growing on his forehead; the blood had thickened to a kind of jelly. He struggled up. Ottilie sat back on her heels and sighed: "Faugh!"

I took him in my arms again and carried him to the house. We must have looked like an illustration from a Victorian novelette, marching forward across the swallow-swept lawn: had Ottilie her hands clasped to her breast? Michael turned his face resolutely away from me. On the steps he wriggled and made me put him down. Charlotte opened the door—and for a moment seemed about to step back hurriedly and shut it again. Ottilie said: "Oh he's all right," and glared at the child. I left them. My lunch had congealed into its own fat.

An hour later Ottilie came to the lodge again. Yes, yes, he was fine, nothing broken, the little brat. She apologised for bringing him to me: mine had been the nearest door. "I'm glad," I said, not knowing quite what I meant. She shrugged. She had put on lipstick. "I got

a fright," she said. We stood awkwardly, looking at
things, like people on a railway platform trying to think
of how to say a definitive goodbye. The sunlight died
in the window and it began to rain. A kind of bubble
swelled suddenly in my breast and I put my hands on
her shoulders and kissed her. There was a fleck of dried
blood on my wrist. Her lipstick tasted like something
from childhood, plasticine, or penny sweets. When I
stepped back she simply stood frowning, and moving
her lips, as if trying to identify a mysteriously familiar
taste.

"I think he dislikes me," I said.

"What? No. He was embarrassed."

"Do children get embarrassed?"

"Oh yes," she said softly, and looked at me at last,
"Oh yes."

It's strange to be offered, without conditions, a body
you don't really want. You feel the most unexpected
things, tenderness of course, but impatience too, curiosity, a little contempt, and something else the only
name for which I can find is sadness. When she took off
her clothes it was as if she were not merely undressing,
but performing a far more complex operation, turning
herself inside out maybe, to display not breast and bum
and blonde lap, but her very innards, the fragile lungs,
mauve nest of intestines, the gleaming ivory of bone,

and her heart, passionately labouring. I took her in my arms and felt the soft shock of being suddenly, utterly inhabited.

I was not prepared for her gentleness. At first it seemed almost a rebuff. We were so quiet I could hear the rain's whispered exclamations at the window. In the city of the flesh I travel without maps, a worried tourist: and Ottilie was a very Venice. I stumbled lost in the blue shade of her pavements. Here was a dreamy stillness, a swaying, the splash of an oar. Then, when I least expected it, suddenly I stepped out into the great square, the sunlight, and she was a flock of birds scattering with soft cries in my arms.

We lay, damp and chill as stranded fish, until her fingers at the back of my neck gave three brisk taps and she sat up. I turned on my side and gazed in a kind of fond stupor at the two folds of flesh above her hip bone. She put on her trousers and her lumpy sweater and padded into the kitchen to make tea. Our stain on the sheet was the shape of a turtle. Grey gloom settled on my heart. I was dressed when she came back. We sat on the bed, in our own faintly ammoniac smell, and drank the strong tea from cracked mugs. The day darkened, the rain was settling in.

"I suppose you think I'm a right whore," she said.

It was contingency from the start, and it stayed that way. Oh, no doubt I could work up a map of our separate journeys to that bed. There would be a little stylised tree on it and a tumbling Cupid, and an X in crimson ink marking a bloodstain, and pretty slanted blue lines indicating rain. But it would be misleading, it would look like the cartography of love. What can I say? I won't deny her baroque blonde splendour touched me. I remember her hands on my neck, the violet depths of her eyes, her unexpectedly delicate pale feet, and her cries, the sudden panic of her coming, when she would clutch me to her, wet teeth bared and her eyelids fluttering, like one falling helplessly in a dream. But love?

She burrowed into my life at the lodge with stealthy determination. She brought prints clipped from glossy magazines and pinned them over the bed, film stars, Kneller's portrait of Newton, the *Primavera*. Flowers began to sprout around me in jam jars and tin cans. A new teapot appeared, and two cups, of fine bone china, each with an identical crack. One day she arrived lugging an ancient radio that she had salvaged from the garage. She played with it for hours, gliding across the stations, mouth a little open, eyes fixed on nothing, while Hungarian disc jockeys or Scots trawlermen gabbled in her ear, and the day waned, and the little green light on the tuning panel advanced steadily into the encroaching darkness.

I think more than sex, maybe even more than love, she wanted company. She talked. Sometimes I suspected she had got into bed with me so that she could talk. She laid bare the scandals of the neighbourhood: did I know the man in Pierce's pub was sleeping with his own daughter? She recounted her dreams in elaborate detail; I was never in them. Though she told me a lot about the family I learned little. The mass of names and hazy dates numbed me. It was all like the stories in a history book, vivid and forgettable at once. Her dead parents were a favourite topic. In her fantasy they were a kind of Scott and Zelda, beautiful and doomed, hair blown back and white silk scarves whipping in the wind as they sailed blithely, laughing, down the slipstream of disaster. All I could do in return was tell her about Newton, show off my arcane learning. I even tried reading aloud to her bits of that old Galileo article of mine—she fell asleep. Of course we didn't speak much. Our affair was conducted through the intermediary of these neutral things, a story, a memory, a dream.

I wondered if the house knew what was going on. The thought was obscurely exciting. The Sunday high teas became an institution, and although I was never comfortable, I confess I enjoyed the sexual freemasonry with its secret signs, the glances and the covert smiles, the way Ottilie's stare would meet and mingle with mine across the table, so intensely that it seemed there must grow up a hologram picture of a pair of tiny lovers cavorting among the tea things.

Our love-making at first was curiously innocent. Her generosity was a kind of desperate abasing before

33

the altar of passion. She could have no privacy, wanted none, there was no part of her body that would hide from me. Such relentless giving was flattering to begin with, and then oppressive. I took her for granted, of course, except when, exhausted, or bored, she forgot about me. Then, playing the radio, brooding by the stove, sitting on the floor picking her nose with dreamy concentration, she would break away from me and be suddenly strange and incomprehensible, as sometimes a word, one's own name even, will briefly detach itself from its meaning and become a hole in the mesh of the world. She had moments too of self-assertion. Something would catch her attention and she would push me away absentmindedly as if I were furniture, and gaze off, with a loony little smile, over the brow of the hill, toward the tiny music of the carnival that only she could hear. Without warning she would punch me in the chest, hard, and laugh. One day she asked me if I had ever taken drugs. "I'm looking forward to dying," she said thoughtfully; "they give you that kind of morphine cocktail."

I laughed. "Where did you hear that?"

"It's what they give people dying of cancer." She shrugged. "Everybody knows that."

I suppose I puzzled her, too. I would open my eyes and find her staring into the misted mirror of our kisses as if watching a fascinating crime being committed. Her hands explored me with the stealthy care of a blind man.

Once, gliding my lips across her belly, I glanced up and caught her gazing down with tears in her eyes. This passionate scrutiny was too much for me, I would feel something within me wrapping itself in its dirty cloak and turning furtively away. I had not contracted to be known as she was trying to know me.

And for the first time in my life I began to feel my age. It sounds silly, I know. But things had been happening to me, and to the world, before she was born. The years in my life of her non-being struck me as an extraordinary fact, a sort of bravura trick played on me by time. I, whose passion is the past, was discovering in her what the past means. And not just the past. Before our affair—the word makes me wince—before it had properly begun I was contemplating the end of it. You'll laugh, but I used to picture my deathbed: a hot still night, the lamp flickering and one moth bumping the bulb, and I, a wizened infant, remembering with magical clarity as the breath fails this moment in this bedroom at twilight, the breeze from the window, the sycamores, her heart beating under mine, and that bird calling in the distance from a lost, Oh utterly lost land.

"If this is not love," she said once in that dark voice of hers, for a moment suddenly a real grown-up, "Jesus if this isn't love then what is!"

The truth is, it seemed hardly anything—I hear her hurt laugh—until, with tact, with deference, but immovably, another, a secret sharer, came to join our somehow, always, melancholy grapplings.

MICHAEL'S birthday was at the end of July, and there was a party. His guests were a dozen of his classmates from the village school. They were all of a type, small famished-looking creatures, runts of the litter, the girls spindle-legged and pigtailed, the boys watchful under cruel haircuts, their pale necks defenceless as a rabbit's. Why had he picked them, were they his only friends in that school? He was a blond giant among them. While Charlotte set the table in the drawing-room for their tea, Ottilie led them in party games, waving her arms and shouting, like a conductor wielding an insane orchestra. Michael hung back, stiff and sullen.

I had gone up to the house with a present for

him. I was given a glass of tepid beer and left in the kitchen. Edward appeared, brandishing a hurley stick. "We've lost a couple of the little beggars, haven't seen them, have you? Always the same, they go off and hide, and start dreaming and forget to come out." He loitered, eyeing my glass. "You hiding too, eh? Good idea. Here, have a decent drink." He removed my beer to the sink and brought out tumblers and a bottle of whiskey. "There. Cheers. Ah."

We stood, like a couple of timid trolls, listening to the party noises coming down the hall. He leaned on the hurley stick, admiring his drink. "How are you getting on at the lodge," he said, "all right? The roof needs doing—damn chilly spot in the winter, I can tell you." Playing the squire today. He glanced sideways at me. "But you won't be here in the winter, will you."

I shrugged; guess again, fella.

"Getting fond of us, are you?" he said, almost coyly.

Now it was my turn to exercise the sideways glance.

"Peace," I said, "and quiet: that kind of thing."

A cloud shifted, and the shadow of the chestnut tree surged toward us across the tiled floor. I had taken him from the start for a boozer and an idler, a lukewarm sinner not man enough to be a monster: could it be a mask, behind which crouched a subtle dissembler, smiling and plotting? Impossible. But I didn't like that look in his eye today. Had Ottilie been telling secrets?

"I lived there one time, you know," he said.

"What—in the lodge?"

"Years ago. I used to manage the nurseries, when Lotte's father was alive."

So: a fortune hunter, by god! I could have laughed.

He poured us another drink, and we wandered outside into the gravelled yard. The hot day hummed. Above the distant wood a hawk was hunting.

Lotte.

"Still doing this book of yours?" he said. "Used to write a bit of poetry, myself." Ah, humankind! It will never run out of surprises. "Gave it up, of course, like everything else." He brooded a moment, frowning, and the blue of the Dardanelles bloomed briefly in his doomy eyes. I watched the hawk circling. What did I know? Maybe at the back of a drawer somewhere there was a sheaf of poems that unleashed would ravish the world. A merry notion; I played with it. He went into the kitchen and fetched the bottle. "Here," handing it to me, "you do the honours. I'm not supposed to drink this stuff at all." I poured two generous measures. The first sign of incipient drunkenness is that you begin to hear yourself breathing. He was watching me; the blue of his eyes had become sullied. He had a way, perhaps because of that big too-heavy head, of seeming to loom over one. "You're not married, are you?" he said. "Best thing. Women, some of them..." He winced, and thrust his glass into my hand, and going to the chestnut tree began unceremoniously to piss against the trunk, gripping that white lumpy thing in his flies with the finger and thumb of a delicately arched hand, as if it were a violin bow he held. He stowed it away and took up his hurley stick. "Women," he said again; "what do you think of them?"

I didn't like the way this was going, old boys together, the booze and the blarney, the pissing into the wind. In a minute we'd be swapping dirty stories. He took back his drink, and stood and watched me, beetling o'er his base. He had violence in him, he would never let it out, but it was all the more unsettling that way, clenched inside him like a fist.

"They're here to stay, I suppose," I said, and produced a laugh that sounded like a stiff door opening. He wasn't listening.

"It's not their fault," he said, talking to himself. "They have to live too, get what they can, fight, claw their way. It's not their fault if . . ." He focused on me. "Succubus! Know that word? It's a grand word, I like it." To my horror he put an arm around my shoulder and walked me off across the gravel into the field beyond the chestnut tree. The hurley he still held dangled down by my side. There were little tufts of vulpine fur on his cheekbones and on the side of his neck behind his earlobe. His breath was bad. "Did you see in the paper," he said, "that old woman who went to the Guards to complain that the man next door was boring holes in the wall and putting in gas to poison her? They gave her a cup of tea and sent her home, and a week later she was found dead, holes in the bloody wall and the fellow next door mad out of his mind, rubber tubes stuck in the wall, a total lunatic." He batted me gently with his stick. "It goes to show, you should listen to people, eh? What do you think?" He laughed. There was no humour in it. Instead, a waft of woe came off him that made me miss a step. What was he asking of me?—for he was asking something. And then I noticed an odd fact. He was hollow. I mean physically, he was, well, hollow. Oh, he was built robustly enough, there was real flesh under his tweeds, and bones, and balls, blood, the lot, but inside I imagined just a greyish space with nothing in it save that bit of anger, not a fist really, but just a tensed configuration, like a three-dimensional diagram of stress. Even on the surface too something was lacking, an essential lustre. He seemed covered in a fine fall of dust, like a stuffed bird in a bell jar. He had not been like this when I came here. The discovery was peculiarly gratifying. I had been a little afraid of him before. We turned back to the house. The bottle, half-empty, stood on the windowsill. I disengaged his arm and filled us another shot. "There," I said. "Cheers. Ah."

A station wagon, the back bristling with flushed children, headed down the drive. At the gate it pulled up with a shriek of brakes as a long sleek car swept in from the road and without slowing advanced upon the house. "Jesus, Mary and Joseph," Edward said: "The Mittlers." He retreated into the kitchen. The visitors

were already at the front door, we heard their imperious
knock and then voices in the hall.

"I'll be going," I said.

"No you don't." He reached out a hand to grab
me, draining his glass at the same time. "Family, interesting, come on, meet," and with a hanged man's grimace thrust me before him down the hall.

They were in the drawing-room, a youngish
woman in grey and a fat man of fifty, and two pale little
girls, twins, with long blonde candle-curls and white
socks.

"This is Bunny," Edward said, "my sister, and
Tom, Tom Mittler; Dolores, here, and Alice."

One twin pointed a thumb at the other. "*She's* Alice."

Tom Mittler, fingering his cravat, nodded to me
and mumbled something, with a fat little laugh, and
then performed the curious trick of fading instantly on
the spot. His wife looked me up and down with cool
attention. Her skirt was severely cut, and the padded
shoulders of her jacket sloped upward, like a pair of trim
little wings. An impossible pillbox hat was pinned at an
angle to her tight yellow curls. It was hard to tell if her
outfit were the latest thing, but it gave her an antiquated
look that was oddly sinister. Her mouth was carefully
outlined with vermilion glaze, and looked as if a small
tropical insect had settled on her face. Her eyes were
blue, like Edward's, but harder. "My name is Diana,"
she said. Edward laughed. She ignored him. "So you're
the lodger?"

"I'm staying in the lodge, yes," I said.

"Comfy there?" and that little red insect lifted its wing-tips a fraction. She turned away. "Is there any chance of a cup of tea, Charlotte? Or is it too much trouble?"

Charlotte, poised outside our little circle, suddenly stirred herself. "Yes, yes, I'm sorry—"

"I'll get it," Ottilie said, and slouched out, making a face at me as she went past.

Bunny looked around, bestowing her painted smile on each of us in turn. "Well!" she said, "this is nice," and extracted from her hat its long steel pin. "But where's the birthday boy?"

"Hiding," Edward murmured, and winked at me.

"Full of fun today," his sister said. She looked at the hurley stick still in his hand. "Are you coming from a game, or going to one?"

He waggled the weapon at her playfully. "Game's just starting, old girl."

"Haw!" Tom Mittler said, and vanished again instantly.

There was a small commotion as Ottilie brought in the tea on a rickety trolley. Michael came after her, solemnly bearing the teapot like a ciborium. At the sight of him Bunny gave a little cry and the twins narrowed their eyes and advanced; their father made a brief appearance to hand him his present, a five-pound note in a brown envelope. Bunny shrugged apologetically: "We didn't have time to shop. Ottilie, this is lovely. Cake and all! Shall I be mother?" The visitors disposed themselves around the empty fireplace and ate with gusto, while the tenants of the house hovered uncertainly, temporarily dispossessed. Edward muttered something and went out. Bunny watched the door closing behind him and then turned eagerly to Charlotte. "How is he?" eyes alight, dying to know, tell me tell me.

There was a moment's silence.

"Oh," Charlotte said, "not . . . I mean . . . all right, you know."

Bunny put down her cup and sat, a study in sorrow and sympathy, shaking her head. "You poor thing; you *poor* thing." She looked up at me. "I suppose you know about . . . ?"

"*No*," Charlotte said swiftly.

Bunny put a hand to her mouth. "Oops, sorry."

Edward came back bearing the whiskey bottle. "Here we are: now, who's for a snort?" He paused, catching something in the silence. Then he shrugged. "Well I am," he said, "for one. Tom: you? And I know *you* will." He poured Mittler and me a measure each. Tom Mittler said: "Thanky voo." Edward lifted his glass. "What will we drink to?"

"August the twenty-seventh," Bunny said, quick as a flash.

They turned blank looks on her. I remembered.

"Mountbatten?" I said. One of their dwindling band of heroes, cruelly murdered. I was charmed: only *they* would dare to make a memorial of a drawing-room tea party. "Terrible thing, terrible."

I was soon disabused. She smiled her little smile at me. "And don't forget Warrenpoint: eighteen paras, *and* an earl, all on the one day."

"Jesus, Bunny," Edward said.

She was still looking at me, amused and glittering. "Don't mind him," she said playfully, "he's a West Brit, self-made. *I* think we should name a street after it, like the French do. The glorious twenty-seventh!"

I glanced at her husband, guzzling his tea. Someone had said he was a solicitor. He had a good twenty years on her. Feeling my eye on him he looked up, and smoothed a freckled hand on his scant sandy hair and said cheerfully: "She's off!"

Bunny poured herself another cup of tea, smirking.

"It's dead men you're talking about," Edward muttered, with the sour weariness of one doing his duty by an argument that he has long ago lost.

"There's nothing wrong with this country," Bunny said, "that a lot more corpses like that won't cure." She lifted her cup daintily. "Long live death! Is this your own cake, Charlotte? Scrumptious."

I realised, with the unnerving clarity that always comes to me with the fifth drink, that if there were to be a sixth I would be thoroughly drunk.

One of the twins suddenly yelped in pain. "Mammy mammy he *pinched* me!"

Michael looked at us from under sullen eyebrows, crouched on the carpet like a sprinter waiting for the off. Bunny laughed. "Well pinch him back!" The girl's face crumpled, oozing thick tears. Her sister watched her with interest.

"Michael," Edward rumbled, and showed him the hurley stick. "Do you see this . . . ?"

Ottilie left to make more tea, and I followed her. Outside the kitchen windows the chestnut tree murmured softly in its green dreaming. The afternoon had begun to wane.

"Quite a lady," I said, "that Diana."

Ottilie shrugged, watching the kettle. "Bitch," she said mildly. "She only comes here to . . ."

"What?"

"Never mind. To gloat. You heard her with Charlotte: *you poor thing.*" She made a simpering face. "Make you sick."

The kettle, like a little lunatic bird, began to whistle shrilly.

"He's not that bad," I said, "is he, Edward?"

She did not answer. We returned to the drawing-room. A dreamy sort of silence had settled there. They sat, staring at nothing, enchanted figures in a fairy tale. Bunny glanced at us as we came in and a flicker of interest lit her hard little eyes. She would be good at ferreting out secrets. I moved away from Ottilie.

"You're quite at home, I see," Bunny said.

"People are kind," I answered, and tried to laugh. My legs were not working properly. Bunny lifted a quizzical eyebrow. "That's true," she said. She was

thinking. I lost interest in her. Edward knocked the
bottle against my glass. His face was ashen. His breath
hit me, a warm brown cloud. I looked at Charlotte, the
only dark among all these fair. She sat, back arched and
shoulders erect, slim arms extended across her lap, her
pale hands clasped, a gazelle. Poor thing. My heart wob-
bled. The bruised light of late afternoon conjured other
days, their texture felt but they themselves unremem-
bered. I seemed about to weep. Edward cracked his
fingers and sat down to the scarred upright piano. He
played atrociously, swaying his shoulders and crooning.
Bunny tried to speak over the noise but no one listened.
Michael sat in the middle of the floor, playing sternly
with the toy car I had given him. I took Ottilie's hands
in mine. She stared at me, beginning to laugh. We
danced, stately as a pair of tipsy duchesses, round and
round the faded carpet. Bunny fairly ogled us. His rep-
ertory exhausted, Edward rose and led Charlotte pro-
testing to the piano. She fingered the keys in silence for
a moment and then began hesitantly to play. It was a
tiny delicate music, it seemed to come from a long way
off, from inside something, and I imagined a music box,
set in motion by a chance breeze, a slammed door,
launching into solitary song in its forgotten spot in the
corner of an attic. I stopped to watch her, the dark glossy
head, the pale neck, and those hands that now, instead
of Ottilie's, seemed to be in mine. Light of evening, the
tall windows—Oh, a gazelle! Ottilie moved away from
me, and knelt beside Michael. The toy car had fallen

over drunkenly on its side, whirring. He narrowed his eyes. He had been trying all this time to break it. Edward took up the mangled thing and examined it, turning it in his thick fingers with a bleared brutish lentor. I looked at the three of them, Ottilie, the child, the ashen-faced man, and something stirred, an echo out of some old brown painting. Jesus, Mary and Joseph. They receded slowly, slowly, as if drawn away on a piece of concealed stage machinery. And then all faded, Bunny, her fat husband, their brats, the chairs, the scattered cups, all, until only Charlotte and I were left, in this moment at the end of a past that now was utterly revised. I hiccupped softly. On the piano lid there was an empty glass, a paper party hat, a browning apple core. These are the things we remember. And I remember also, with Ottilie that night moaning in my arms, feeling for the first time the presence of another, and I heard that tiny music again, and shivered at the ghostly touch of pale fingers on my face.

"What's wrong," Ottilie said, "what is it?"

"Nothing," I answered, "nothing, nothing."

For how should I tell her that she was no longer the woman I was holding in my arms?

Next morning along with the hangover came inevitably the slow burn of alarm. Had I said anything, let slip some elaborate gesture? Had I made a fool of myself?

I recalled Bunny smirking, the tip of her little nose twitching, but that had been when I was still with Ottilie. Even so sharp an eye surely would not have spotted my solitary brief debauch by the piano? And later, in the dark, there had been no one to see me, save Ottilie, and she did not see things like that. Like what? In every drunkenness there comes that moment of madness and euphoria when all our accumulated knowledge of life and the world and ourselves seems a laughable misapprehension, and we realise suddenly that we are a genius, or fatally ill, or in love. The fact is obvious, simple, beyond doubt: why have we not seen it before? Then we sober up and everything evaporates, and we are again what we are, a frail, feckless, ridiculous figure with a headache. But in vain I lay in bed that morning waiting for reality to readjust itself. The fact would not go away: I was in love with Charlotte Lawless.

I was astonished, of course, but there was too a familiar shiver of fright and not wholly unpleasurable disgust. It was like that moment in a childhood party game when, hot and flustered, every nerve-end an eye, you whip off the blindfold to find that the warm quarry quivering in your clasped arms is not that little girl with the dark curls and the interestingly tight bodice whose name you did not quite hear, but a fat boy, or your convulsed older sister, or just one of Auntie Hilda's mighty mottled arms. Or a middle-aged woman, emphatically married, with middle-aged hands, and wrin-

kles around her eyes, and the faint beginnings of a
moustache, who had spoken no more than twenty
words to me and who looked at me as if I were, if not
transparent, then translucent at least. There it was, all
the same, sitting in bed with me, still in its party frock,
with an impudent smile: love.

The secret pattern of the past months was now
revealed. I saw myself that first day in the doorway of
the lodge offering her a month's rent, I stumbled again
down the grassy bank to the glasshouse, sat in her
kitchen in sunlight watching the shadows of leaves stirring by her hand. I was like an artist blissfully checking
over the plan of a work that has suddenly come to him
complete in every detail, touching the marvellous, still-
damp construct gently here and there with the soft feel-
ers of imagination. Ottilie a sketch, on the oboe, of the
major theme to come, Edward at once the comic relief
and the shambling villain of the piece, Michael a Cupid
still, the subtlety of whose aim, however, I had under-
estimated. Even the unbroken fine summer weather was
a part of the plot.

Of course there were to be times when the whole
thing would seem a delusion. I would remark the fact
that the actual life I led—burnt cutlets, the bathroom
to be cleaned—was far from that ideal which somehow
I would manage to think I was leading: the quiet scholar
alone with books and pipe and lamplight, lifting melancholy eyes now and then to the glossy block of night
in the window and sighing for *die ferne Geliebte*. When

Ottilie came to me I saw myself as one of those tragic gentlemen in old novels who solace themselves with a shopgirl, or a little actress, a sort of semi-animate doll with childlike ways and no name, a part for which my big blonde girl was hardly fitted. But then, as suddenly as they had come, the doubts would depart, and the dream would take wing again into the empyrean, when I saw her coming up from the glasshouse with flowers in her arms, or glimpsed her lost in thought behind a tall window in which was reflected one tree and a bronze cloud. Once, listening idly to the shipping forecast on the radio, I saw her come out on the steps in the tawny light of evening and call to the child, and even still always I think of her when I hear the word *Finisterre*.

In moments like that you can feel memory gathering its material, beady-eyed and voracious, like a demented photographer. I don't mean the big scenes, the sunsets and car crashes, I mean the creased black-and-white snaps taken in a bad light, with a lop-sided horizon and that smudged thumb-print in the foreground. Such are the pictures of Charlotte, in my mind. In the best of them she is not present at all, someone jogged my elbow, or the film was faulty. Or perhaps she was present and has withdrawn, with a pained smile. Only her glow remains. Here is an empty chair in rain-light, cut flowers on a workbench, an open window with lightning flickering distantly in the dark. Her absence throbs in these views more powerfully, more poignantly than any presence.

When I search for the words to describe her I can't find them. Such words don't exist. They would need to be no more than forms of intent, balanced on the brink of saying, another version of silence. Every mention I make of her is a failure. Even when I say just her name it sounds like an exaggeration. When I write it down it seems impossibly swollen, as if my pen had slipped eight or nine redundant letters into it. Her physical presence itself seemed overdone, a clumsy representation of the essential she. That essence was only to be glimpsed obliquely, on the outer edge of vision, an image always there and always fleeting, like the afterglow of a bright light on the retina.

If she was never entirely present for me in the flesh, how could I make her to be there for me in the lodge, at night, in the fields on my solitary rambles? I must concentrate on things impassioned by her passing. Anything would do, her sun hat, a pair of muddied wellingtons standing splay-footed at the back door. The very ordinariness of these mementoes was what made them precious. That, and the fact that they were wholly mine. Even she would not know their secret significance. Two little heart-shaped polished patches rubbed on the inner sides of those wellingtons by her slightly knock-kneed walk. The subtle web of light and shade that played over her face through the slack straw of the brim of her hat. Who would notice such things, that did not fix on her with the close-up lens of love?

Love. That word. I seem to hear quotation marks around it, as if it were the title of something, a stilted sonnet, say, by a silver poet. Is it possible to love someone of whom one has so little? For through the mist now and then I glimpsed, however fleetingly, the fact that what I had of her was hardly enough to bear a great weight of passion. Perhaps call it concentration, then, the concentration of the painter intent on drawing the living image out of the potential of mere paint. I would make her incarnate. By the force of my unwavering, meticulous attention she would rise on her scallop shell through the waves and *be*.

I did nothing, of course, said nothing, made no move. It was a passion of the mind. I had given up all pretence of work on the book. You see the connection.

I wondered if she were aware of being so passionately watched. Now and then I thought I caught her squirming, as if she had felt my slavering breath brush her flesh. She had a way of presenting me suddenly with unbidden bits of fact, like scraps thrown down to divert the attention of a dog that she feared might bite her. She would turn her head, consider for a moment my right shoulder, or one of my hands, with that strange blank gaze, and say: My father imported that tree from South America. And I would nod pensively, frowning. I learned the oddest things from her. Why a ha-ha is so called. That Finland was the first European country to give women the vote. Occasionally I could link these obscure pronouncements to something I had said or asked days ago, but mostly they were without discernible connection. Having spoken, she would go on gazing at me for a moment longer, as if waiting for some large sign of my acknowledgment that she was solid, that, see, she knew things, like real people do—or just that she was too dry for this dangerous dog to bother biting.

I recall one Saturday, when she was driving into town to deliver stuff from the nurseries, and I asked her for a lift. It was raining, the fields a speeding blur beyond the misted windows. We were past the village when she took her foot off the pedal and let the car bump slowly to a stop. "Puncture," she said. But she did not get out. We looked in silence at a wild apple tree shimmering before us in the streaming windscreen. The wheels on my side had climbed the grass verge, and everything was slightly crooked. There was no puncture. A strange moment, I remember it, the rain, the sound of the rain, the worn sticky feel of the car seat. She took off her spectacles, and a strand of hair fell across her face. What was she thinking about? I did not like the way she wore her glasses on a cord, it made her look matronly. An old harridan within me suddenly muttered: *She's forty if she's a day*, and was immediately silenced. A minute went by. I rolled down my window and let in the smell of woodbine and wet earth. Charlotte rubbed the fogged windscreen with a fingertip. "Perhaps we should go back," she said, and then, looking at my knees: "Edward is not well." The sibyl had spoken. I nodded, a puzzled priest of the shrine. What was expected of me? Whatever it was I could not give it, and she turned with vague helplessness to the plants and punnets of fruit stacked on the back seat. Her eyes, what colour were her eyes? I can't remember! She started up the car. We drove on.

Thus, always, it would teeter on the brink of being something.

———————— ⬭ ⬭ ————————

At first I was afraid I'd give the game away, snatch up her hand and kiss it, or get drunk again and fall at her feet bawling, something like that. But of course I wouldn't. I was like a young bride who has rushed home to tell hubby that the pregnancy is confirmed, only to go suddenly shy and strange at the sight of familiar things, his hat, that new sofa, the kitchen sink. In the midst of the old life I hugged this brand-new secret to my breast. It gave me a curious sense of dignity, of quiet wisdom. Is this what love is really for, to lend us a new conception of ourselves? My voice sounded softer to me, my every action seemed informed by a melancholy grandeur. My smile, faintly flecked with sadness, was a calm benediction upon the world.

I had feared too I might reveal myself before Ottilie, by showing a sudden coldness. But in fact, I was if anything fonder of her now. I even warmed toward Edward; I fairly doted (at a safe distance) on the child. They were nearer to Charlotte, in the commonplace world of breakfasts and bedtimes, than I could ever be. And they were the keepers of that most precious thing, her past. That they could not hope to achieve the proximity to her that I did, in my love, was something for which they could not be blamed, but only pitied. I spent hours, a smiling spider, weaving webs to trap them into talking about her, so that it would be always they who appeared to have brought up the subject. The hardest part was to keep them from straying on to other things. Then I was forced to take desperate action, and, elaborately casual, would jump in with: But what you were saying about Charlotte, it was interesting, did she really never have a boyfriend before Edward? And a red-hot coal of panic would briefly glow behind my breastbone when Ottilie paused, and glanced at me, struck I suppose by the incongruity of putting together such words as *Charlotte* and *boyfriend*.

Being a man with a secret was a full-time role. Sometimes I almost lost sight of the beloved herself in the luxuriant abundance of my mission. When Ottilie was in my arms I was careful not to speak, for fear of crying out the wrong name—but there were moments too when I was not sure which was the right one, moments even when the two became fused. At first I had conjured Charlotte's presence to be only a witness to the gymnastics in my narrow bed, to lean over us, Ottilie and me, with the puzzled attention of a pure spirit of the night, immune herself to the itch of the flesh yet full of tenderness for these sad mortals struggling among the sheets, but as time went on this ceased to be enough, the sprite had to fold her delicate wings, throw off her silken wisps, and, with a sigh of amused resignation, join us. Then in the moonlight my human girl's blonde hair would turn black, her fingers pale, and she would become something new, neither herself nor the other, but a third—Charlottilie!

There was a fourth, too, which was that other version of myself which stood apart, watching the phenomenon of this love and my attendant antics with a wry smile, puzzled, and at times embarrassed. He it was who continued to, I won't say love, but to value Ottilie, her gaiety and generosity, her patience, the mournful passion that she lavished on me. Was there, then, another Ottilie as well, an autochthonous companion for that other I? Were all at Ferns dividing thus and multiplying, like amoebas? In this spawning of multiple selves I seemed to see the awesome force of my love, which in turn served to convince me anew of its authenticity.

Perhaps this sense of displacement will account for the oddest phenomenon of all, and the hardest to express. It was the notion of a time out of time, of this summer as a self-contained unit separate from the time of the ordinary world. The events I read of in the newspapers were, not unreal, but only real *out there*, and irredeemably ordinary; Ferns, on the other hand, its daily minutiae, was strange beyond expressing, unreal, and yet hypnotically vivid in its unreality. There was no sense of life messily making itself from moment to moment. It had all been lived already, and we were merely tracing the set patterns, as if not living really, but remembering. As with Ottilie I had foreseen myself on my deathbed, now I saw this summer as already a part of the past, immutable, crystalline and perfect. The future had ceased to exist. I drifted, lolling like a Dead Sea swimmer, lapped round by a warm blue soup of timelessness.

I even went back to the book, in a way. I needed something on which to concentrate, an anchor in this world adrift. And what better prop for the part of hopeless lover than a big fat book? Sitting at my table before the window and the sunlit lilacs I thought of Canon Koppernigk at Frauenburg, of Nietzsche in the Engadine, of Newton himself, all those high cold heroes who renounced the world and human happiness to pursue the big game of the intellect. A pretty picture—but hardly a true one. I did little real work. I struck out a sentence or two, rearranged a paragraph, corrected a few solecisms, and, inevitably, returned again to the second, and longer, of those two strange letters to Locke, the one in which N. speaks of having sought *a means of explaining the nature of the ailment, if ailment it be, which has afflicted me this summer past*. The letter seemed to me now to lie at the centre of my work, perhaps of Newton's too, reflecting and containing all the rest, as the image of Charlotte contained, as in a convex mirror, the entire world of Ferns. It is the only instance in all his correspondence of an effort to understand and express his innermost self. And something *is* expressed, understood, forgiven even, if not in the lines themselves then in the spaces between, where an extraordinary and pitiful tension throbs. He wanted so much to know what it was that had happened to him, and to say it, as if the mere saying itself would be redemption. He mentions, with unwonted calm, Locke's challenge of the absolutes of space and time and motion on which the picture of the mechanistic universe in the *Principia* is founded, and trots out again, but without quite the old conviction, the defence that such absolutes exist in God, which is all that is asked of them. But then suddenly he is talking about the excursions he makes nowadays along the banks of the Cam, and of his encounters, not with the great men of the college, but with tradesmen, the sellers and the makers of things. *They would seem to have something to tell me; not of their trades, nor even of how they conduct their lives; nothing, I believe, in words. They are, if you will understand it, themselves the things they might tell. They are all a form of saying*—and there it breaks off, the rest of that page illegible (because of a scorch mark, perhaps?). All that remains is the brief close: *My dear Doctor, expect no more philosophy from my pen. The language in which I might be able not only to write but to think is neither Latin nor English, but a language none of whose words is known to me; a language in which com-*

monplace things speak to me; and wherein I may one day have to justify myself before an unknown judge. Then comes that cold, that brave, that almost carven signature: *Newton.* What did he mean, what was it those commonplace things said to him, what secret did they impart? And so I sat in the shadow of lilacs, nursing an unrequitable love and reading a dead man's testament, trying to understand it.

WHATEVER I had felt for Ottilie in the beginning, there was not much left now save lust, and irri-
tation, and a kind of grudging compassion. She sensed
the change, of course, and began to probe it. She came
to the lodge more often, as if to test my endurance. She
said she wanted to stay all night, she didn't care what
they thought at the house. Then she would look at me,
not listening to my excuses, only watching my eyes and
saying nothing. I began cautiously to try to disengage
myself. I talked a lot about freedom. Why tie ourselves
down? This summer would end. She was too young to
throw away the best moments of her life on a dry old
scholar. Her eyes narrowed. I too wondered what I was
getting at—but no, that's not true, I knew damn well.

It was devious, and heartless, and horribly pleasurable. Who knows the sweet stink of power like the disenchanted lover renouncing all claim to loyalty? I pictured her known flesh soiled by some faceless other, yet gloried in the knowledge that I need only give the reins the faintest twitch and she would come running back to me, awash in her lap.

I look back on myself in those days, and I do not like what I see.

We spent hours in bed, entire afternoons seeped away into the sheets. We invented new positions, absurd variations that left us gasping, our sinews aquiver. She had me bind her hands and tie her to chairs, to the legs of the bed. We made love on the floor, against the walls. If Michael had not been liable to pop up from the undergrowth she would have dragged me naked out into the grass to do it. When she bled we devised a whole manual of compromises. No witch could have worked at her dark art more diligently than she.

Sometimes this frenzied sorcery of the senses frightened me. Squatting before her with my face in her lap, staring in silent fascination at the brownish frills and violet-tinted folds of her sex, I would suddenly feel something blundering away from me, an almost-creature of our making, damaged and in pain, dragging a blackened limb along the floor and screaming softly. It was an image of guilt, of my shame and her desperation, the simple fear that she would get pregnant, and of things too more deeply buried. Its counterpart, light to that dark, was the pale presence of a third always with us, who was my private conjuring trick. "Look at me!" Ottilie would say, "Look at me when we're doing it, I want you to see me!" I looked at her, that was easy. But after these bouts of ghostly troilism I hardly had the nerve to face Charlotte.

Curiously, I seemed to see Ottilie more clearly now than ever before. Receding from me, she took on the high definition of a figure seen through the wrong end of a telescope, fixed, tiny, complete in every detail. Anyway, from the first I had assumed that I understood her absolutely, so there was no need to speculate much about her. I suppose that is why I had never asked her about the child. It seems incredible to me, now, that I didn't. She could not have been more than sixteen when he was born. Who was the father—some farmhand, or a local young buck, a wandering huckster perhaps who had come to the door one day and captivated her with his patter and his wicked eye? That she was the mother I never doubted. But she said nothing, and neither did I, and as the weeks and months went on the unasked question became faded, like one of those huge highway signs so worn by being looked at that its message has gone mute.

I don't remember when it was exactly that this skeleton began to rattle its bones with a new urgency in the Lawless cupboard. It might have been the day of Michael's party, when I turned starry-eyed from the piano and saw the three of them, Ottilie and Edward and the child, posed in a north light by the window like models for the *Madonna of the Rocks*, but probably I'm being fanciful. It was later, anyway, before I began to brood in earnest, when my love for Charlotte was demanding other, grosser conspiracies to keep it company. Then everything was in flux, and anything was possible. One Sunday, for instance, Ottilie casually remarked that she had skipped the family excursion to Mass to be with me. Mass? They were *Catholics?* My entire conception of them had to be revised.

And then there was the day she played that extraordinary trick on me. She came to the lodge, out of breath and grinning slyly. Edward and Charlotte were in Dublin, Michael was at school. "Well?" she said, hands in her pockets, shoulders hunched, smiling and swaying, imitating some film star; "you've never seen *my* room." We walked up the drive under the sycamores. It was an eighteenth-century day, windswept and bright, the distances all small and sharply defined, as if painted on porcelain. The trees were that dry tired green that heralds their turning. Prompted by intimations of autumnal sadness I took her hand, and remembered suddenly, vividly, as I still can, the first time she had shown herself to me naked. In the hall she stopped and looked around her at the clock, the mirror, the hurley stick in the umbrella stand. She sighed. "I hate this place," she said, and I kissed her open mouth with a sweet sense of sin. The sight of the child's room sobered us; we crept past. At the next door she hesitated, biting her lip, and then threw it open. The bed was a vast squat beast with curlicues and wooden knobs. There was a smell of stale clothes and face-powder. In a corner the flowered wallpaper was bubbled on a damp patch. Is there anything more cloyingly intimate than the atmosphere of other people's bedrooms? The window looked across the lawn to the lodge. "I see you can keep an eye on me," I said, and laughed gloomily, like a travelling salesman in a brothel. She cast a vague glance at the window. She was already halfway out of her clothes. There was a black hair on the pillow, like a tiny crack in enamel.

We lay for a long time without stirring, in silence, desireless. A parallelogram of sunlight was shifting stealthily along the floor beneath the window. Against the pale sky I watched a flock of birds wheeling silently at a great height over the fields. A memory from childhood drifted up, paused an instant, showing the gold of its lazily beating fins, and then went down again, without breaking the surface. I kissed the damp thicket of her armpit. She stroked my cheek. She began to say something, stopped. I could feel her trying it out in her head. I waited; she would say it. There are moments like that, sunlit and still, when the worst and deepest fear of the heart will drift out with the dreamy innocence of a paper skiff on a pond.

"You've lost interest," she said, "really, haven't you."

A little cloud, like a white puff of smoke, appeared

in the corner of the window. Summer is the shyest season.

"Why do you say that?"

She smiled. "So you'll tell me it's not true." She had a way of looking at me, tentative and cool, as if she had spotted a small fault in the pupil of my eyes, and were wondering whether or not she should mention it.

"It's not true."

"Could I take that to mean, now, that you love me?"

"Oh, all this *love*," I said wearily, "I'm weary of it."

"All what love?" pouncing, as if with the winning line of a word game.

"See that cloud?" I said. "That's love. It comes along, drifts across the blue, and then . . ."

"Goes."

Silence.

She sat up, hugging the sheet to her breast. "Well," she said briskly, "will I tell you something?" Her face above me, foreshortened, glazed by reflected sunlight, was for a moment an oriental mask. "This is not my room."

"What? Then whose . . . ?" She grinned. "Jesus Christ, Ottilie!" I leapt up like a scalded cat and stood, naked and aghast, staring at her. She laughed. "You should see your face," she said, "you're all red."

"You are mad." It was an extraordinary sensation: disgust, and a kind of panic, and, incredibly, tumescence. I turned away, scrabbling for my clothes. I felt as if I had been turned to glass, as if the world could shine through me unimpeded: as if I were now a quicksilver shadow in someone else's looking-glass fantasy. What had possessed her, to bring me here? Was I perhaps not the only one who played at plots of sexual risk and renunciation? "I'm going for a piss," she muttered, and flung herself from the room. I dressed, and stood at bay, breathing through my mouth in order not to smell the flat insinuating odour of other people's intimacies. All I could think of was Edward's clumsiness, the way his sausage fingers fumbled things. A book would erupt in his hands like a terrified bird, pages whirring, dust-jacket flapping, while he looked away, talking over his shoulder, until the thing with a crisp crack dropped lifeless, its spine broken, and then he would peer at it with a kind of guilty puzzlement. How could I be doing this, to a man like that. Doing what? I realised I felt as I would feel if I had cuckolded him. Ottilie came back. She sat down on the side of the bed and clasped herself in her arms. "I'm cold."

"For Christ's sake, Ottilie—"

"Oh, what harm is it?" she said. "They'll never know." She looked up at me resentfully, pouting, a big naked child. "I thought you might like to . . . here . . . that's all."

"You're *mad*."

"No I'm not. I know things," slyly, "I could tell you things."

"What does that mean?"

"You'll have to find out for yourself, won't you? You don't know anything. You think you're so clever, but you don't know a thing."

I slapped her face. It happened so quickly, with such a surprising, gratifying precision, that I was not sure if I had not imagined it. She sat quite still, then lifted a hand to her already reddening cheek. She began to cry, without any sound at all. "I'm sorry," I said. I left the room and closed the door carefully behind me, as if the slightest violence would scatter the shards of something in there shattered but still all of a precarious piece. Outside, in the ordinary light of afternoon, I still felt unreal, but at least I could breathe freely.

That afternoon was to contaminate everything. I looked at the others with a new surmise, full of suspicions. They were altered, the way someone you have known all your life will be altered after appearing, all menace and maniacal laughter, in a half-remembered dream. Up to now they had been each a separate entity. I hadn't thought of them as husband and wife, mother, son, niece, aunt— aunt!—but now suddenly they were a family, a closed, mysterious organism. Amazing questions occurred to me. What really did they mean to each other? What did Charlotte feel for the child? Did Edward and she resent orphan Ottilie's presence? Were the women jealous of each other, did they circle each other warily, as Edward and I did? And what did they all think of me, how did they behave when I was not there, did they talk about me? What did they see when they looked at me?—a kind of shadow, a trick of light, a ghost grown familiar of whom no one is frightened anymore? I felt a new shyness in their presence, an awkwardness. I was like an embarrassed anthropologist realising that what he had for months taken to be the ordinary muddle of tribal life is really an immense intricate ceremony, in which the tiniest gesture is foreordained and vital, in which he is the only part that does not fit.

All questions came back to the one question: why had she chosen *that* room? Impulse? A simple prank? Or did she have some intimation of the delicate dance I was doing with Charlotte in my mind *(I thought you might like to ... here ...)*? And if so, did Charlotte—my god, did Charlotte herself suspect, did she feel when I came near something reach out and touch her timidly, the moist pale limb of my longing? There are people you cannot, will not imagine *doing it*, but now I could not stop myself speculating on the nightworld of Ferns. Why did Charlotte and Edward have no children? Which of them was ... ? The names wove a web of confusion in my mind. I began to have lurid dreams in which the four of them slipped and slithered, joining and sundering, exchanging names, faces, voices, as in some obscene surrealist fantasy. I lay in bed in the lodge and tried to imagine Edward here, younger, less besotted, watching the old man Charlotte's father, waiting for him to die, planting his claim to Ferns by seducing the daughter, perhaps on this very mattress . . . I sat up, as suddenly as I had that day in that other bed. I was sweating. The girl my fevered imaginings had put in Edward's arms was not Charlotte. Away in the woods a night bird was singing. Sixteen, for god's sake, she was only sixteen!

Impossible.

The weather broke. I wakened in the middle of the night to a noise of shipwreck, a smashed mast, doomed sailors crying in the wind. In the morning when I looked out the kitchen window the scenery was rearranged. The storm had brought down a tree. It lay, a great stranded corpse, in a tangle of brambles and twisted branches not a foot from the gable end of the lodge. The day had a hangdog air, mud everywhere, and granite clouds suspended over the fields. Snails crunched under my tread. The summer was over.

Edward came down the drive in a shabby raincoat and a ridiculous tweed hat. "Some night, eh?" He peered at the fallen tree. "By Christ that was a close one, nearly got you." I found it hard to look him in the face, and studied his extremities instead, the brown brogues, twill trousers, the cuffs of his raincoat. Was I imagining it, or was he shrinking; his clothes seemed made for someone a shade fuller. He looked ghastly, ashen-faced and blotched by the cold. Another hard night. Where did he do his drinking? Once or twice I had seen him sloping into the hotel bar in the village, but latterly he had been keeping to the house. Perhaps he kept a cache of bottles stowed under floorboards, at the back of the linen cupboard, as domesticated drunks are said to do. Or maybe he drank openly, turning his back on Charlotte's sad gaze. "Planted that tree myself," he said, "Lotte and me, one day." He looked up, smiling sheepishly, shrugging. "That's the summer gone." Something came off him, a kind of mute plea. For what, for sympathy? I was afraid he would start maundering again about women, life and love. A warm gush of contempt rose like gorge in my gullet. He felt it, for he laughed, shaking his head, and said: "You're a hard man." For a moment I could not make out the emphasis, then I realised that *he* was sympathising with *me*. By god! I stared at him—on your knees, cur!—but he only laughed again, and turned away.

Going up to the house that evening, I met in the hall a large red-faced man in a blue suit. He winked at me, and ran a finger down his fly. Above our heads the lavatory was still noisily recovering from his visit. "Bad old weather," he said, jauntily. We went together into the drawing-room; tea was being served there in the visitor's honour. Edward leaned against the mantelpiece in his squire's outfit of tweed and twill, one hand in his trousers pocket wriggling like a conjuror's rabbit. I tried to see him as a seducer. It was surprisingly easy. Younger, hair slicked down, creeping up on her. Give us a kiss? I'll tell Charlotte. Ah you wouldn't now. Let go! Yum yum, lovely titties . . . Charlotte was looking at me in mute dismay: she had forgotten it was Sunday. Tough. Visitors were rare, I wasn't about to miss this one. She came at us quickly, her hands out, like someone stepping in to stop a fight. "Mr Prunty is in the seed business." I looked at Mr Prunty with interest. He winked again.

"Have a drink," said Edward.

Charlotte turned quickly. "The tea is ready!"

He shrugged. "Oh, right."

Ottilie and the child came in.

Mr Prunty was a great talker, and a great eater; his laughter made the table tremble. He was trying to buy the nurseries. I suspect he had already a hold on the Lawlesses. When business matters were mentioned he grew ponderously coy. I studied him. I had seen him before: he was a type. His money made, he was after style now, and class. He gazed upon the Lawlesses with a kind of fond indulgence. He loved them, a ripe market. There would be no stopping him. Gently, lovingly, he would relieve them of Ferns. Eventually he would become a patrician, change his name, maybe, breed a brood of pale neurotic daughters to sit in this room doing needlepoint and writing hysterical novels. "It's a fair offer," he said seriously, glancing round the table, a forkful of food suspended before him. "I think it's a fair offer." And he laughed.

They sat looking back at him, glumly, a little stupidly even, like a small band of supplicants come from the sacked city to beg for clemency before the emperor's tent. I had not spoken to Ottilie since the afternoon in the Lawlesses' bedroom. Edward coughed.

"Well—" he began.

Charlotte, who had been gazing at the large blue man with hypnotic fascination, dragged herself out of her trance.

"He's writing, you know," she said to Mr Prunty, pointing at me, "a book, he is. On Newton. The astronomer."

All eyes turned to me, as if I had that moment descended from the sky into their midst.

"Is that right now," Mr Prunty said.

Charlotte's look pleaded with me. "Aren't you?"

I shrugged. "I *was*." They waited. I was blushing. "I seem to have given it up..."

"Oh?" Ottilie put in, icily bright. "And what are you doing instead?"

I would not look at her.

"Yes," said Mr Prunty, after a pause. "Well as I was—"

"Given it up?" Charlotte said. With her sorrowing

73

eyes, pale heart-shaped face, those hands, she might have
stepped out of a Cranach garden of dark delights.

"Like Newton," I said. "He gave up too."

"Did he?"

"It's not the money that's the point," Edward was
saying, "it's not the main thing," and Mr Prunty, trim-
ming the fat from a piece of ham, pursed his lips, and
pretended to be trying not to smile.

"Yes," I said, "his work, his astronomy, everything. He was fifty; he went a little mad."

"I didn't know that," she said. Michael looked
around cautiously and put the jammy blade of his knife
into his mouth. "Why was that?"

"Ferns is a family affair," Edward said grumpily,
"there's a tradition here."

"Because—"

"Stop that!" Ottilie snapped. Michael slowly removed the knife from his mouth, looking at her.

"Oh true, true," said Mr Prunty smoothly, "the
Graingers have been in this house a long time."

Charlotte, a hand to her naked throat, gave a tiny
shudder. O Isaac, make haste to help me!

"Because he had to have certain absolutes," I said,
look at me, keep looking at me, "certain absolutes of
of of, of space, time, motion, to found his theories on.
But space, and time, and motion," beats, soft beats, soft
heartbeats, "can only be relative, for us, he knew that,
had to admit it, had to let them go, and when they

went," O my darling, "everything else went with them." Ah!

A vast dark cloud sailed into the window.

"Well," said Prunty, routed finally, "I've made my offer, I hope you'll consider it." My lap was damp. Charlotte, as if nothing at all had happened, turned to him coolly and said: "Of course, thank you."

There was some more chat, the weather, the crops, and then he left. Charlotte saw him out. "Bloody gombeen man," Edward said, and yawned. Under the table Ottilie's foot touched mine, retreated, and then came back without its shoe. I suppose she had caught a whiff of rut, and thought the trail led to her. Charlotte returning stopped in the doorway. "Was that lightning?" We turned to the window expectantly. Rain, grey light, a trembling bough. Why do I remember so clearly these little scenes? Because they seemed somehow arranged, as certain street scenes, in quiet suburbs, on dreamy summer evenings, will seem arranged, that postbox, the parked van, one tree in its wire cage, and a red ball rolling innocently into the road down which the lorry is hurtling. A tremendous clap of thunder broke above our heads. "By Christ," Edward said mildly. He turned to Charlotte. A glass of whiskey had appeared in his hand out of nowhere.

"Well?" he said. "What do you think?" She shook her head. "You'll have to sell, you know," he said, "sooner or later."

There was a silence, and once again I had that sense

of them all turning away from me toward some black awful eminence that only they could see.

"We," Charlotte said, so softly I hardly heard it; "*we*, you mean."

———————————————⟨⟩———————————————

I listened to them fighting all evening long, doors slamming, the radio switched full on and as suddenly silenced, and Edward shouting between pauses in which I pictured Charlotte in tears, her face a rain-washed flower lifted imploringly to his. More than once I started to go up to the house, with some wild idea of calling him out, and then subsided helplessly, fists like caricatures clenched before me. The rain stopped, and late sunlight briefly filled the garden, and through the drenched evening an incongruous blackbird began to sing. I felt vaguely ill. A knot of nerves seethed in my stomach. At last I heard the front door bang, and the car bumped down the drive and sped towards town. I drank a glass of brandy and put myself to bed. I was still awake when there came a knock at the door. I leapt up. But it was only Ottilie. She smiled in mock timidity. "Am I allowed to come in?" I said nothing, and poured her a brandy. She watched me, still smiling, and biting her lip. "Listen I'm sorry," she said, "about the other day. It was a stupid—"

"Forget it. I'm sorry I hit you. There. Cheers." I sat on the sofa, pressing the glass to my still heaving stomach. I nodded in the direction of the house. "Fireworks."

"He's drunk," she said. She was wandering about aimlessly, looking at things, her hands thrust in her pockets. "I had to get out. She's just sitting there, doped to the gills, doing the martyr as usual. It's hard to have sympathy all the time . . . " She looked at me: "You know?"

The light was fading fast. She switched on a lamp, but the bulb blew out immediately, fizzing. "Jesus," she said wearily. She sat down at the table and thrust a hand into her hair.

"What's going on," I said, "are they going to sell the place?"

"They'll have to, I suppose. They're not too happy with old Prunty. He'll get it, though, he's rotten with money."

"What will you do, then?"

"I don't know." She chuckled, and said, in what she called her gin-and-fog voice: "Why don't you make me an offer?—Oh don't look so frightened, I'm joking." She rose and wandered into the bedroom. I could hear the soft slitherings as she undressed. I went and stood in the doorway. She was already in bed, sitting up and staring before her in the lamplight, her hands clasped on the blanket, like an effigy. She turned her face to me. "Well?" Why was it that when she took off her clothes, her face always looked more naked than the rest of her?

"He's not much of a salesman," I said.

"Edward? He was different, before."

"Before what?"

She continued to gaze at me. I suppose I looked a little strange, eyes slitted, jaw stuck out; suspicion, anger, jealousy—jealousy!—itches I could not get at to scratch. She said: "Why are you so interested, all of a sudden?"

"I wondered what you thought of him. You never mention him."

"What do you want me to say? He's sad, now."

I got into bed beside her. That blackbird was still singing, in the dark, pouring out its heedless heart. "I'll be leaving," I said. She was quite still. I cleared my throat. "I said, I'll be leaving."

She nodded. "When?"

"Soon. Tomorrow, the weekend, I don't know." I was thinking of Charlotte. Leaving: it was unreal.

"That's that, then." Her face was a tear-stained blur. I took her in my arms. She was hot and damp, as if every pore were a tiny tear-duct. "I want to tell you," she said, after a time, "when you hit me that day and walked out, I lay in their bed for ages making love to myself and crying. I kept thinking you'd come back, say you were sorry, get a cold cloth for my face. Stupid."

I said: "Who is Michael's father?"

She showed no surprise. She even laughed: was that all I could say? "A fellow that used to work here," she said.

"What was his name?"

"I don't remember."

"What became of him?"

"He went away. So did the girl. And Charlotte adopted the child. She couldn't have any, herself."

No. *No*.

"You're lying."

But she wasn't really listening, her ear was turned to the steady trickle of misery that had started up inside her. She laid her forehead against my cheek. "You know," she said, "sometimes I think you don't exist at all, that you're just a voice, a name—no, not even that, just the voice, going on. Oh god. Oh no," furious with herself, yet powerless to stop the great wet sobs that began to shake her, "Oh *no*," and wailing she came apart completely in my arms, grinding her face against mine, her shoulders heaving. I was aghast, I was—no, simply say, I was surprised, that's worst of all. Behind her, darkness stood at the window, silent, gently inquisitive. She drew herself away from me, her face averted. "I'm sorry," she said, gasping, "I'm sorry, but I've never given myself like this to anyone before, and it's hard," and the sobs shook her, "it's *hard*."

"There there," I said, like a fool, helplessly, "there there." I felt like one who has carelessly let something drop, who realises too late, with the pieces smashed all around him, how precious a thing it was, after all. A flash of lightning lit the window, and the rain started up again with a soft whoosh. She wiped her nose on the back of her hand. The tears still flowed, as if there would be no end, but she was no longer aware of them. "I suppose you're sick and tired of me," she said, and lay down, and turned on her side, and was suddenly asleep, leaving me alone to nurse my shock and my cold heart.

WE MUST assume that Edward did go that night into town, and not to the village, as was later to be suggested. The evidence against the latter possibility is twofold. First, there was the direction in which I had heard him drive away. Had he been headed for the village, the sound of the car would have faded quickly as it dropped below the brow of the hill; instead of which, it was audible for a considerable time, a fact consistent with the motor travelling westward, along the main road, the slope of which is much less pronounced than that of the hill road, leading to the village. Second, there is the quite considerable amount of drink which, it would later be obvious, he had consumed. At that stage the publicans of the village, both in the hotel, and in the public houses with which the place is generously endowed, knew better than to serve him the endless double whiskeys which he would demand.

However, his going to town—to coin a phrase—will not account for the considerable lapse of time between closing time (11:30 p.m., summer hours) and his return to Ferns at approximately 2:30 a.m. As to what occurred in those "lost" hours, we can only speculate. Did he meet a friend (did he *have* any friends?) to whose house they might have repaired? The town does not boast a bawdy-house,* therefore that possibility can be eliminated. The quayfront then, the parked car, its lights aglow, the radio humming forlornly to itself, and from within the darkened windscreen the stark suicidal stare? Could he have sat there, alone, for some three hours? Perhaps he slept. One would wish him that blessing.

I can't go on. I'm not a historian anymore.

The first thing I noticed when I woke was that Ottilie was gone. The bed was warm, the pillow still damp from her tears. Then I heard the car, labouring up the drive in first gear. I must have dropped back to sleep for a moment, the voices raised in the distance seemed part of a dream. Then I opened my eyes and lay listening in the darkness, my heart pounding. The silence had the quality of disaster: it was less a silence than an aftermath. I went to the window. Lights were coming on in the house, one after another, as if someone were

---

*I have since learned that this contention is mistaken; cf Polkolski, F. X., *Interface Tribal Situations in Southeast Ireland: a structuralist study* (M. I. T. 1980).

running dementedly from switch to switch. I pulled on trousers and a sweater. The night was pitch-black and still, smelling of laurel and sodden earth. The grass tickled my bare ankles. The car was slewed across the drive, like a damaged animal, its engine running. The front door of the house stood open. There was no one to be seen.

I found Edward in the drawing-room. He was sitting unconscious on the floor with his back against the couch, his head lolling on a cushion, his hands resting palm upward at his sides. A mandala of blood-streaked vomit was splashed on the carpet between his splayed legs. The crotch of his trousers was stained where he had soiled himself. I stood and gaped at him, disgust and triumph jostling in me for position. Triumph, oh yes. Suddenly, through opposing doors, Charlotte and Ottilie swept in, like mechanical figures in a clock tower. They saw me and stopped. "I heard voices," I said. Charlotte blinked. She wore an old plaid dressing-gown. Her feet were bare. Less Cranach now than El Greco. We were quite still, all three, and then everyone began to speak at once.

"I couldn't get through," Ottilie said.

Charlotte put a hand to her forehead. "What?"

"There was no reply."

"Oh."

"We'll have to—"

"Did you ring the right—"

"What?"

83

In the hall a hand appeared on the stairs, a small bare foot, an eye.

"I'll have to go into town," Ottilie said. "Christ." She looked at me. Her face was still raw from weeping. I turned away. I turned away. "Get back to bed, you!" she cried, and the figure on the stairs vanished. She went out, slamming the door, and in a moment we heard the car depart. Gravel from the spinning tyres sprayed the window. *That wall, see, down there.* Charlotte sighed. "She's gone for . . . " She thought a moment, frowning; " . . . for the doctor." She walked about the room as in a dream, picking up things, holding them for a moment, as if to verify something, and then putting them down again. Edward belched, or perhaps it was a groan. She paused, and stood motionless, listening; she did not look at him. Then she went to the switch by the door and carefully, as if it were an immensely complicated and necessary operation, turned off the main lights. A lamp on a low table by the couch was still burning. She crossed the room and sat down on a high-backed chair, facing the window. It all had the look of a ritual she had performed many times before. Something, the lamp-light perhaps, the curious toylike look of things, the helpless gestures meticulously performed, stirred an ancient memory in me of another room, where, a small boy, I had played with two girl cousins while above our heads adult footsteps came and went, pacing out the ceremony of someone's dying.

"Is it raining, I wonder," Charlotte murmured. I

think she had forgotten I was there. I went forward softly and stood behind her. In the black window her face was reflected. I looked down at the pale defenceless parting of her hair; in the opening of her dressing-gown I could see the gentle slope of a breast. How can I describe to you that moment, in lamplight, at dead of night, the smell of vomit mingled with the milky perfume of her hair, and that gross thing sitting there, grotesque and comic, like a murdered pavement artist, and no world around us anymore, only the vast darkness, stretching away. Everything was possible, everything was allowed, as in a mad dream. I could feel her warmth against my thighs. I looked at her reflection in the glass; my face must be there too, for her.

"Mrs Lawless," I said, "this can't go on, you can't be expected to put up with this." My voice was thick, a kind of fat whine. Tell her something, tell her a fact, a fragment from the big world, a coloured stone, a bit of clouded green glass. Young men of the Ipo tribe in the Amazon basin pledge themselves with the nail parings of their ancestors. Oh god. The first little flames of panic were nibbling at me. "Listen," I said, "listen I'll give you my address, my phone number, so that if ever you want . . . if ever you need . . ." I put my hands on her shoulders, and a hot shock zipped along my nerves, as if it were not cloth, flesh and bone I were holding, but the terminals of her very being, and "Charlotte," I whispered, "Oh Charlotte!" and there was a lump thick as a heart in my throat, and tears in my eyes, and the Ipo drums began to beat, and all over the rain forest lurid birds with yellow beaks and little bright black eyes were screeching.

She stirred, and turned up her face to me, blinking. "I'm sorry," she said, "I wasn't listening. What did you say?"

We heard the car returning. So much for the wall of death. The doctor was an ill-tempered old man, still in his pyjamas, with a raincoat thrown over his shoulders. He glared at me, as if the whole affair were my fault. "Where is he? What? Why in the name of Christ didn't you put him to bed?" Gruff, good with children, old women would dote on him. He knelt down, grunting, and felt Edward's pulse. "Where was he drinking?"

Charlotte began distractedly to cry.

"In the village, probably," Ottilie said. She stood, with her hands behind her, leaning back against the door, her swollen eyes shut. Michael was sitting on the stairs, watching through the banisters. Had he been there to hear me pledge my troth to poor unheeding Charlotte?

The doctor and I, with Ottilie's help, lifted Edward and hauled him up the stairs. He opened his eyes briefly and said something. The smell, the slack feel of him, was horrible.

"Let him sleep," the doctor said, "there's nothing

to be done." He turned to Charlotte, watching from the doorway. "And you, Mrs Lawless, are you all right? Have you your pills?" She continued to look at Edward's head sunk in the pillows. She nodded slowly, like a child. "Try and sleep now." The doctor glanced, inexplicably sheepish, at Ottilie and me—good god, was he in love with Charlotte too? "He'll be all right now. I'll come back in the morning."

Ottilie and I went with him to the door. The night came in, smelling of wet and the distant sea. "Can I drive you back?" I said.

Ottilie pushed past me out on the step. "I'll do it."

"He should be kept an eye on," the doctor said, throwing me a parting scowl. "He'll go down fast, after this."

The gaseous light of dawn was filtering into the garden when she came back. I went outside to meet her. I had stood at the window watching for her, listening breathlessly for a sound from upstairs, afraid to leave, but fearful that she would return and find me indoors, trap me, make me drink tea and talk about the meaning of life. Even at that late stage I was still misjudging her. She came up the steps, hugging herself against the cold, and stopped, not looking at me, swinging the car key. I asked a question about the doctor, for something to say.

"Old fraud," she said, distantly, frowning.

"Oh?"

We were wary as two strangers trapped by a downpour in a shop doorway. A seagull swaggered across the lawn, leaving green arrow-prints in the grey wet of the grass.

"Feeding her that stuff."

She waited; my go.

"What stuff?" I felt like a straight-man.

"Valium, seconal, I don't know, some dope like that. Six months she's been on it. She's like a zombie—didn't you notice?" with a tiny flick of contempt.

"I wondered," I said, "yes."

Wonder is the word all right.

A blood-red glow was swelling among the trees. I felt—I don't know. I was cold, and there was a taste of ashes in my mouth. Something had ended, with a vast soft crash.

"In northern countries they call this the wolf hour," I said. A fact! Pity Charlotte was not there to hear me, learning the trick at last. "What is it he has?"

"Edward?" She looked at me then, with scorn, pityingly. "You really didn't know," she said, "all this time, did you."

"Why didn't you tell me?"

She only smiled, a kind of grimace, and looked away. Yes, a foolish question. I felt briefly like a child, pressing his face against the cold unyielding pane of adult knowingness. *She* was the grown-up. I shrugged, and went down the steps. The seagull flew away, scattering its mewling cries upon the air.

THERE'S not much left to tell. That same morning I packed as many of my belongings as I could carry and locked up the lodge. I left the key in an envelope pinned to the door. I thought of writing a note, but to whom would I have written, and what? I stood in the gateway, afraid Ottilie might see me, and come after me—I could not have borne it—taking a last brief view of the house, the sycamores, that broken fanlight they would never fix. Michael was about. He too had grown, already the lineaments of what he would someday be were discernible in the way he held himself, unbending, silent, inviolably private. He was no longer a Cupid. Not a golden bow and arrow, but a flaming sword would have suited him now. I waved to him tentatively, but he pretended not to see me. I set off down the road to the village. The sun was shining, but too bright; it would rain later. The leaves were turning. Farewell, happy fields!

A long low car came up the hill. I almost laughed: it was the Mittlers. Had Bunny turned her little nose twitching to the wind and caught a whiff of disaster? Maybe Charlotte had called them. What did I know? They passed me by with a toot on the deep-throated horn, gazing at me through the smoked glass, the four of them, like manikins. Bunny noted my bag. Before they were past she had turned to her husband, her mouth working avidly.

On the train I travelled into a mirror. There it all was, the backs of the houses, the drainpipes, a cloud out on the bay, just like the first time, only in reverse order. In the dining-car I met Mr Prunty: life will insist on tying up loose ends. He remembered my face, but not where he had seen it. "Ferns, was it," he cried, "that's it!" and jabbed a finger into my chest. I was pleased. He seemed somehow right: vivid yet inconsequential, and faintly absurd. He spoke of Edward in a whisper, shaking his head. "Has it in the gut, I believe, poor bugger—you knew that?"

"Yes," I said, "I know."

Two letters awaited me at the flat, one calling me to an interview in Cambridge, the other offering me the post here. The contract is for a year only. Was I crazy to come? My surroundings are congenial. There is nothing I could wish for, except, but no, nothing. Spring is a ferocious and faintly mad season in this part of the world. At night I can hear the ice unpacking in the bay, a groaning and a tremendous deep drumming, as if something vast were being born out there. And I have heard gatherings of wolves too, far off in the frozen wastes, howling like orchestras. The landscape, if it can be called that, has a peculiar bleached beauty, much to my present taste. Tiny flowers appear on the tundra, slender and pale as the souls of dead girls. And I have seen the auroras.

Ottilie writes every week. I catch myself listening for the postman panting up the stairs. She once told me, at Ferns, that when she was away from me she felt as if she were missing an arm—but now I seem weighed down by an extra limb, a large awkward thing, I don't know what to do with it, where to put it, and it keeps me awake at night. She sent me a photograph. In it she is sitting on a fallen tree, in winter sunlight. Her gaze is steady, unsmiling, her hands rest on her knees; there is the line of a thigh that is inimitably hers. There is something here, in this pose, this gaze at once candid and tender, that when I was with her I missed; it is I think the sense of her essential otherness, made poignant and precious because she seems to be offering it into my keeping. She's in Dublin now. She abandoned her plan to go to university, and is working in a shop. She feels her life is *only starting*.

Of all the mental photographs I have of her I choose one. A summer night, one of those white nights of July. We had been drinking, she got up to pee. The lavatory was not working, as so often, and she had brought in from the garage, to join her other treasures, an ornate china vessel which she quaintly called the jolly-pot. I watched her squat there in the gloaming, her elbows on her knees, one hand in her hair, her eyes closed, playing a tinkling chamber music. Still without opening her eyes she came stumbling back to bed, and kneeling kissed me, mumbling in my ear. Then she lay down again, her hair everywhere, and sighed and fell asleep, grinding her teeth faintly. It's not much of a picture, is it? But she's *in* it, ineradicably, and I treasure it.

She's pregnant. Yes, the most banal ending of all, and yet the one I least expected. Wait, that's not true. I have a confession to make. That last night in bed with her, when she sobbed in my arms: I told you she went immediately to sleep, but I lied. I could not resist her tear-drenched nakedness, the passionate convulsions of her sobbing. God forgive me. I believe that was when she conceived; she thinks so too. More sentimentality, more self-delusion? Probably. But at least this delusion has a basis in fact. The child is there. The notion of this strange life, secret in its warm sea, provokes in me the desire to live—to live forever, I mean, if necessary. The future now has the same resonance that the past once

94

had, for me. I am pregnant myself, in a way. Supernumerous existence wells up in my heart.

I set out to explain to you, Clio, and to myself, why I had drown'd my book. Have you understood? So much is unsayable: all the important things. I spent a summer in the country, I slept with one woman and thought I was in love with another; I dreamed up a horrid drama, and failed to see the commonplace tragedy that was playing itself out in real life. You'll ask, where is the connection between all that, and the abandoning of a book? I don't know, or at least I can't say, in so many words. I was like a man living underground who, coming up for air, is dazzled by the light and cannot find the way back into his bolt-hole. I trudge back and forth over the familiar ground, muttering. I am lost.

Edward survived the winter. He's very low, bedridden: *you wouldn't know him*, she says. As if I ever did. I remember one day he tried to tell me about dying. Oh not directly, of course. I can't recall what he said, what words he used. The subject was the countryside, farming, something banal. But what he was talking about, I suppose, was his sense of oneness now with all poor dumb things, a horse, a tree, a house, that suffer their

lives in silence and resigned bafflement, and die unre-
marked. I wish I could have erected a better monument
to him than I have done, in these too many pages; but
I had to show you how I thought of him *then*, how I
behaved, so that you would see the cruelty of it, the
wilful blindness.

Of Charlotte she makes no mention. That was only to
be expected. I brood on certain words, these emblems.
Succubus, for instance.

What shall I do? Find that fissure in the rocks, clamber
down again into that roomy and commodious grave? I
hope not. Begin afresh, then, learn how to live up here,
in the light? Something is moving under the ice. Oh,
I'm not in despair, far from it. I feel the spring around
me, the banality of it, the heedless power. Emotions
flourish in these frozen wastes. I stop sometimes, staring
at a white hill with the tender porcelain of the sky behind
it, and I feel such a sense of... of something, I don't
know. All kinds of things appear on that white screen:
a house, a chestnut tree, a dark window with a face
reflected in it. Oh and other things, too many to mention. These private showings seem an invitation. Go
back to Ferns, move in, set up house, fulfil some grand

design, with Ottilie, poor Charlotte, the two boys—for I feel it will be a boy, it must be—become a nurseryman and wear tweeds, talk about the weather, stand around chewing a straw? Impossible. All the same, I *shall* go back. And in the end, it's come to me just this moment, in the end of course I shall take up the book and finish it: such a renunciation is not of this world. Yet I'm wary. Shall I have to go off again, leaving my research, my book and everything else unfinished? Shall I awake in a few months, in a few years, broken and deceived, in the midst of new ruins?

Dublin–Iowa–Dublin
Summer 79–Spring 81